Watersnake

by Anthony Masters

Illustrated by Stephen Player

Contents

Introduction

After Mr Rogers, his swimming coach, died,
Jamie joined Darren's gang.
Now he wishes he hadn't.

Darren is the leader of the gang. He is a vandal and a big bully, who can fight and win.

Darren

Billy

Ed

Billy and Ed suck up to Darren.
They do whatever he says.

Can Jamie stop the gang from wrecking the old swimming pool? First he must face up to his greatest fear, and learn the secret of the watersnake . . .

CHAPTER 1

The Watersnake

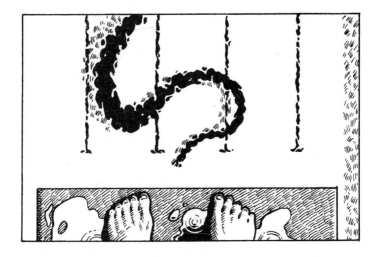

Jamie could see a snake. He blinked. This just couldn't be happening.

He was standing on the top diving-board of Ramsden Road Baths, trying to get his courage up. He had never managed from up here before, and he knew he wouldn't be able to do it now. How could he, with a giant watersnake down there, sliding over the cracked green tiles?

Jamie felt sick. Was he just seeing things in the pool?

He thought of old Mr Rogers, his swimming coach, who had died from a heart attack a couple of months ago. What would he do if he saw a snake underwater?

I've got to dive off here, he told himself. If I don't, I'll be letting Mr Rogers down.

But, as usual, when he looked at the surface of the pool, Jamie shuddered. It was such a long way down. He could see the tiles at the bottom of the water, all wavy and looking like green slime. And now he could see the snake!

Mr Rogers' kind voice echoed in his mind. "Go on, Jamie. Give it a go. The water won't bite you."

A snake might bite, Jamie thought, and started to climb down the steps.

He knelt down on the edge of the pool to see if the snake was still there. How silly – he must have been seeing things.

There was no snake. Only the empty pool.

CHAPTER 2

The Gang

Jamie was in a gang. The other members were Billy, Darren and Ed, all boys of his own age. The day after Jamie thought he saw the snake they all met up in the school playground.

"Let's smash up the pool," said Darren.

"Great idea," replied Billy.

"Count me in," laughed Ed.

"You can't smash up the pool." Jamie was horrified.

"Why not? It's closing next week."

"No reason to smash it up, though," Jamie said. Since he had been dropped from the swimming team he had joined the gang for something to do. Now he wished he hadn't.

They were vandals, the bunch of them – and they loved breaking things up. He was also scared of them. They were bigger than he was.

"You chicken then?" asked Darren.

"Course not," Jamie replied.

"Then you're coming with us," snapped Billy.

"No, I'm not!"

"We'll see," said Darren.

Jamie thought about the snake. He was sure that he had been seeing things. He was also sure that he had to do something to stop the gang smashing up Ramsden Road Baths. The only way he could do that was to go with them – and see what he could do.

They went straight down to the pool after school.

"We'll hide in the filter plant and come out when the pool's closed," said Darren. He was the leader of the gang – a big fair-haired boy who could fight and beat any of them.

Jamie was almost as scared of Darren as the top diving-board.

But not quite.

"I've got some paint sprays – and a couple of hammers," said Ed. "We can go bananas."

"If we make too much noise the police will come." Billy was always more timid.

Jamie said nothing. The closer they got to Ramsden Road Baths the worse he felt. He was sure something awful was going to happen – unless he put a stop to it. But how?

The plan was to have a final swim and then hide. Jamie got changed and walked to the deep end. They haven't done much to mark the closing of the pool, he thought, as he dived in from the spring-board and fast-crawled his way up and down for a few lengths. There should be flags hung out, he thought. Or a speech. But there was no one there – only Joe, the lifeguard who was too old to save anyone.

What would his old coach Mr Rogers have done? He would have been very upset.

Suddenly there was a great deal of splashing. Someone seized him round the neck and ducked him in the shallow end.

Then they ducked him again. He knew it was Darren. He was too strong for Jamie to fight back. So Jamie just let him do what he had to do – which was to duck him for the third time.

When he came up, Darren said, "You're not going to grass us up tonight, are you?"

"You're not to smash up the pool," said Jamie.

Darren looked round carefully. Joe seemed to be asleep and there were no other staff on duty. There weren't even any other swimmers – and the rest of the gang were in the deep end.

Darren grabbed Jamie's arm and hauled it up behind his back in a half-nelson. "You've got to do what I say," he snarled.

Chapter 3

Darren

"You're not to smash up the pool," repeated Jamie. He tried to struggle, but he knew it wouldn't be any good. It wasn't. Darren was always too strong.

"You grass on us – and I'll beat you up."

Jamie knew he would.

"You're going to help us have some fun."

"No."

"Yes, you will." Looking around again, to make sure no one was watching, Darren pulled Jamie's arm higher up his back. "You will, won't you? You'll help us have some fun."

He just couldn't bear the pain any longer. "OK."

"And you won't grass us?"

"No."

"And you'll do what I say."

"Yes."

"All the time."

"Yes!"

Darren let his arm go, ducked him again and swam off, laughing.

Jamie surfaced, almost in tears but determined not to cry. What was he going to do?

If only Mr Rogers was still alive – he would know what to do. The long, thin whistle came that meant the baths were closing. For the last time. Jamie felt sick with worry.

19

Ramsden Road Baths were so old that the cubicles were built down each side of the pool, facing the water. As he changed, Jamie looked down at the water lapping against the sides. He would miss the pool very much. He had spent hours practising when Mr Rogers was alive.

Jamie felt sad. He would never dive off the high board now. He had chickened out once too often. He thought of the watersnake he had seen – or thought he had seen. Wouldn't it be great if it suddenly rose out of the water and swallowed up Darren? But that would be too much to hope for now; anyway, it had obviously been a trick of the light.

As he tied up the laces of his trainers, Jamie wondered how he was going to stop the gang vandalizing Ramsden Road Baths. Billy and Ed weren't too bad, but with Darren around – well, he meant trouble. Big trouble!

CHAPTER 4

The Hiding Place

The lady at the pay desk had gone home and only old Joe was left to lock up the pool for the last time. It was easy for the gang to hide in the filter plant which was behind the diving-board. The room was small and smelt

23

of chlorine, but there was a good place to hide behind the big drum of chemicals. In fact Joe never came near them; they heard his footsteps, heard him click off switches, lock doors – and then there was silence. Even the water in the pool didn't make a sound. Jamie had never heard such a silence; it was scary.

"Let's go," said Billy.

"Come on." Ed couldn't wait.

"No," hissed Darren. "Wait another few minutes – just to make sure the old twit's gone." He was a bully, but he wasn't thick.

"You got the spray-cans?" asked Billy.

"In my bag," replied Darren.

"What about the hammers?" asked Ed.

"In my bag," repeated Darren. "Now shut up, you two."

Something was wrong. He couldn't remember where Jamie was hiding. Could he have slipped out somewhere? "Jamie!" he whispered.

"Yeah?"

"Where are you?"

"Here."

"You ready?"

Jamie didn't reply.

"I said – are you ready?"

"Yes," he replied in a very small voice.

"OK," said Darren after waiting a few more minutes. "Let's go for it."

As they crept out Ed tripped over a bucket and fell to the floor with a fearful clatter. He yelled out in pain.

They stood, half in and half out of the doorway. Waiting.

The pool shimmered like glass. The silence seemed to hang in the air. No one came. Jamie wished they had.

"You total idiot," said Darren.

"I've broken my foot," muttered Ed.

"If it *was* broken," said Darren, "you wouldn't be standing on it, would you?"

"It hurts."

"So it should. Now shut up!"

CHAPTER 5

Vandals

Darren felt around in his bag and produced a hammer for each of them and a can of spray paint. They were all brand new.

"Where did you get this lot?" asked Billy.

"Nicked 'em, didn't I? Now, follow me and let's get stuck in."

They were standing in shadowy darkness but there were a few security lights so they could see what they were doing.

"OK," said Darren, raising his hammer. "It's goodbye Ramsden Road." He brought it down hard on the first of the old cubicles and the wood split at once. To cheers from Ed and Billy he hit it again and there was a terrible tearing sound.

"You lot – get stuck in," he yelled.

With a whoop of joy, Billy and Ed grabbed their hammers and were just about to start bashing when Jamie yelled, "Stop."

Darren turned to him with a nasty grin. "What did you say?"

"I said – stop."

"Yeah?"

"Yeah." Jamie tried to tough it out as Darren put down his hammer and strode towards him. The others watched in suspense. Now he was for it.

"What did you say?"

"I said stop. If you don't – I'll call the police."

Jamie felt bolder now. He was sure that Mr Rogers was watching him.

Darren was close to Jamie now, breathing into his face.

"How will you do that then?"

"Go to the phone."

"Oh yeah?"

"I'm going now."

"You are, are you?" Darren moved even closer, beckoning to the excited Ed and Billy.

"You know what's going to happen to you, don't you?"

"No, I don't," said Jamie. Was Darren going to beat him up?

"You're going in the pool."

Ed and Billy whooped with joy again. They hadn't really wanted to see Jamie knocked out. Darren could be nasty when he wanted to be.

"Oh yes?" asked Jamie, squaring up to him. He just didn't care any longer. He had to protect the pool. Mr Rogers would have wanted him to do that.

"Get him," yelled Darren. "He's going in the pool. Now!"

"Fully dressed?" gasped Billy.

"You bet."

Jamie tried to fight back, but in seconds they had grabbed his arms and legs and thrown him in.

Jamie swam below the surface and

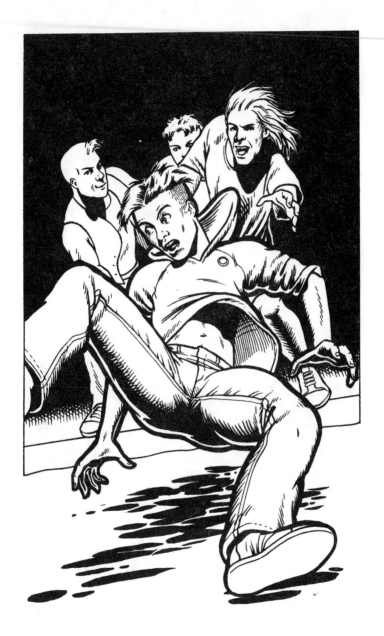

touched the bottom of the pool. He opened his eyes underwater, quite at home. In fact, if he didn't have to breathe, he would have been quite happy to stay there. He pulled off his trainers, just as Mr Rogers had taught him, and swam strongly, still underwater, to the deep end, where he bobbed up again.

Darren was standing there grinning, but Ed and Billy looked scared.

"Let him out," said Billy.

"Only if he promises not to make any more trouble," said Darren.

"He'll drown!" yelled Ed.

"Him? He's like a fish. He should have been a fish. Don't you remember – he was taught by old man Rogers. Right little goodie-goodie. Rogers was just an old twit."

Jamie dived underwater again. He couldn't bear to hear Darren being nasty about Mr Rogers.

CHAPTER 6

Fangs

Jamie opened his eyes and saw the watersnake, coiled up on the green tiles at the bottom of the pool. It was uncoiling itself, its forked tongue was slipping in and out of its mouth and he could see its fangs. Its eyes looked angry.

Jamie was terrified.

At amazing speed the watersnake streaked off towards the shallow end. It was a kind of greeny blue but Jamie could also see through it. He broke surface. The gang had walked down to the shallow end.

Darren and Ed were attacking the changing cubicles again and Billy was spray-painting the walls.

Jamie clung on to the side, wondering if he should shout a warning. As the watersnake reached the shallow end, the water started to boil as if it was hot. But instead it turned freezing cold.

Jamie clambered out, his jeans and sweatshirt clinging to him.

"Oi!" he shouted.

But Darren didn't turn round. "You learnt your lesson?" he yelled over his shoulder.

"No," said Jamie quietly. "But you'll be learning something yourself any moment now."

"What was that?"

Billy was the first to spot the watersnake as it reared out of the pool. It was almost twice as long now, its green head looming over the gang and its forked tongue crackling with electricity.

Jamie looked on with amazement turning to fear.

Billy screamed in terror as the watersnake towered over them. "Look!"

"What now?" Darren turned round – and his mouth fell open. Sweat streamed down his

face and he screamed again and again. Ed
made no sound. He just stared, became
deadly pale and began to shake all over.

The water started to slop over the side of the pool. The snake, glittering like cold steel, seemed part of the water itself. Yelling now, Ed was the first to run into a cubicle and try to shut himself in. But quick as a flash the head of the watersnake was round the door and there was a horrible sucking sound. The

door crashed wide open as Ed was pulled
backwards at great speed and dumped in the
pool.

Standing on the other side, his clothes
dripping, Jamie didn't know what to do. Was
the snake going to drown the gang? What
was it going to do to him?

Now it was Billy's turn. He froze for a moment as the snake reared up again. Jamie could see that it was part of the water, and could rise as high as it liked.

Down in the deep end of the pool Ed clung on to the side. He was crying, yelling for help, saying he'd do anything if someone would get him out. Billy began to run all round the sides of the pool while Darren dropped his hammer on the ground and looked on in absolute horror. It was almost as if the giant watersnake was playing with Billy, its beady eyes and huge body revolving slowly. Suddenly Billy made a dash for the swing doors. He got there all right and was soon outside, making for the entrance. He's got away, thought Jamie, not knowing whether to be glad or sorry.

Suddenly the watersnake put its head down and shot out like a huge wave, crashing through the doors, flooding the corridor and

winding itself round Billy's waist like a
tornado. As it dragged him back, the doors to
the pool sprang open and Billy was hurled
into the pool to join the screaming Ed. Now it
was Darren's turn.

CHAPTER 7

Games

Darren had been thinking. Desperately. But he hadn't come up with any ideas, so when the huge head of the watersnake turned towards him, all he could think of doing was heading back to the filter plant.

Once again the giant watersnake looked as if it was playing with him. It let him get into the room and slam the door. Jamie heard Darren locking it behind him.

But it was no good. The watersnake hurled itself down the pool at an amazing speed and then poured over the side, its head flattening, its whole body becoming a sheet of water that poured under the doors of the filter plant. Jamie heard a howl of fear from Darren.

There was a long silence – and the door burst
open backwards with a loud crash. The
watersnake had Darren in its watery jaws. It
rose up as high as the top board and threw its
third and final victim into the deep end.

The snake slithered back, stirring the water into a whirlpool as it began to spin round and round. Darren, Billy and Ed were in the middle, circling so fast that they kept going underwater, yelling for help every time they came up for air.

At first Jamie thought, 'Serve them right!' But soon he became more and more worried as the water whirled faster and faster. They're going to drown, he thought. What on earth can I do?

"Dive," whispered the voice in his mind.

"Who's that?" he asked, startled.

"Dive," the voice repeated. It was familiar, but Jamie couldn't think who the voice belonged to.

CHAPTER 8

Angry Water

Then he knew who it was. Of course it couldn't be true, but the voice belonged to Mr Rogers.

"Dive, Jamie." It was Mr Rogers. But not speaking out loud. The voice was inside his mind.

"The water's angry. It's protecting the pool."

"But what about the snake?"

"The water made the snake. Show it who's boss – like I did. Show the water you're not scared, Jamie. Then the snake will go away."

He looked at the whirlpool. It seemed to be going even faster and the boys were not coming up for air very often now. He had to do something.

"Dive from where?" But he knew where.

He couldn't see the head of the watersnake now, just the whirlpool as it flashed round and round.

"The top board. Where else?"

He knew he couldn't delay any longer or the gang would drown. So Jamie ran down the side of the pool, wondering if he should take any of his sopping wet clothes off.

"Help," yelled Darren as he surfaced briefly, only to be sucked down again.

Jamie knew he didn't have time to do anything – but dive!

He raced up to the top board, and as he climbed, the whirlpool seemed to go even faster. Wouldn't the giant watersnake ever grow tired?

Now he was on the board – just the place where he usually froze and couldn't move. But now Jamie didn't even hesitate. He ran, dived and soared down towards the lashing water.

As he went below the surface, he could see
the angry coils of the snake. But as he
surfaced, the water suddenly calmed down,
the whirlpool went away and the giant snake
completely disappeared. The pool slopped and
gurgled and surged – and Darren, Ed and Billy

managed to swim to the side, where they clung, choking and gasping.

The pool was flat and calm now, and except for the gang's gasping there was complete silence. Jamie swam lazily to the ladder and hauled himself out.

He would have to explain his wet clothes at home. At least two of the cubicles were badly damaged and one wall had been partly spray-painted. They would also have to be very careful about how they left the building. But the Ramsden Road Baths had been saved.

He walked round to the gang, who were still clinging to the side of the pool.

"Don't let it come back," whimpered Ed.

"No more snake," pleaded Billy. He was so scared that he had gone back to talking like a baby again.

"You've got to tell it to go away," wept Darren. He seemed more scared than any of them.

"It'll come back if we do any more damage," said Jamie.

"We won't," chorused Billy and Ed. "We promise we won't."

"The demolition men will be here soon," grumbled Darren, getting his wits together

again. "Don't see what we did wrong."

"I do," said Jamie.

As Jamie soggily squelched his way down the corridor of Ramsden Road Baths he heard Mr Rogers' voice in his mind again.

"Well done, Jamie. I always knew you could do it."